the ADVENTURES of
ROBIN
HOOD

Retold by

Joanne Mattern

SCHOLASTIC INC.

ISBN 978-1-338-30378-0

10 9 8 7 6 5 4 3 2 1 18 19 20 21 22

Printed in the U.S.A. 40

First printing 2018

Book design by Jennifer Rinaldi

Contents

How Robin Hood Came to Be an Outlaw

IN MERRY ENGLAND in times of old, when King Henry the Second ruled the land, there lived in Sherwood Forest, near Nottingham Town, a famous outlaw named Robin Hood. No archer ever lived who could shoot an arrow with such skill, nor were there ever such men as those who roamed with him. Merrily they dwelled within Sherwood Forest, suffering neither care nor want, but passing the time in merry games of archery, living upon the king's deer.

Not only Robin but also his band were outlaws and dwelled apart from other men, yet they were beloved by the country people, for no one ever came to Robin for help in time of need and went away with an empty hand.

Now I will tell how Robin Hood became an outlaw.

When Robin was a youth of eighteen, strong of muscle and bold of heart, the Sheriff of Nottingham proclaimed a shooting match and offered a prize to whoever could shoot the best. Robin took his stout yew bow and a score of arrows and started off from his home in Locksley Town through Sherwood Forest to Nottingham.

It was at the dawn of day in the merry month of May, when hedges are green and flowers bloom in the meadows. Robin whistled as he trudged along, thinking of Maid Marian and her bright eyes, for at such times a youth's thoughts turn to the lady he loves the best.

As Robin walked with a brisk step and a merry whistle, he came upon some foresters seated beneath a great oak tree, making merry with food and drink. One of them called out to Robin, "Where are you going, little lad, with your one-penny bow and your farthing shafts?"

Robin grew angry, for no one likes to be taunted for being young.

"My bow and arrows are as good as yours. I go to the shooting match at Nottingham Town, where I will shoot with the best."

The man said, "Ha! Why, boy, you boast of standing up with good stout men at the match. You can scarcely draw your bow!"

At this Robin grew angry. "Look," said he. "I see a herd of deer at the glade's end. I will wager twenty pounds that I can strike one from this distance."

"Done!" cried the man who had spoken first. "I wager you will not strike any deer this day."

Robin took his yew bow in his hand. Placing the tip at his instep, he strung it, nocked an arrow, and, raising the bow, drew the gray goose feather to his ear. The next moment, the bowstring rang and the arrow sped down the glade, as a sparrow hawk skims in a northern wind. High leaped the noblest deer of all the herd, only to fall dead, reddening the path with his heart's blood.

"Ha!" cried Robin. "How do you like that shot, good fellow? It looks like I have won this wager."

Then all the foresters were filled with rage, and he who had spoken first and lost the wager was the angriest of all.

"No," he cried. "Don't you know that you have killed the king's deer, and by the laws of our gracious lord and sovereign King Henry you should die for your crime?" He turned to the others. "Seize him!" he shouted.

Robin, realizing the trouble he was in, ran into the depths of the greenwood. Although he escaped the foresters, all the joy and brightness of that day were gone. He was outlawed because he had poached the king's deer; two hundred pounds were set upon his head as a reward for whoever would bring him to the court of the king. So he came to dwell in the greenwood, which was to be his home for many a year to come, never again to see happy days with the lads and lasses of sweet Locksley Town.

Robin Hood lay hidden in Sherwood Forest for one year, and in that time there gathered around him many others like himself. Some had shot deer in hungry wintertime, when they could get no other food, and had been seen in the act by the foresters but had escaped. Some had been turned out of their inheritances, that their farms might be added to the king's lands in Sherwood Forest. Some had been robbed by a great baron or a rich bishop. All, for one cause or another, had come to Sherwood to escape injustice and oppression.

So that year, one hundred or more good yeomen gathered about Robin Hood and chose him to be their leader and chief. Then they vowed that they would hurt their oppressors, whether baron, bishop, knight, or squire, even as they themselves had been hurt, and from each they would take what had been taken from the poor by unjust taxes or in wrongful fines. But to the poor folk they would give a helping hand in need and would return to them that which had been unjustly taken from them. In time, the people came to praise Robin and his merry men, and to tell many tales of him and of his doings in Sherwood Forest, for they felt him to be one of their own.

Robin Hood Meets Little John

UP ROSE ROBIN HOOD one merry morn when all the birds were singing among the leaves, and up rose his merry men. Robin said, "For fourteen days we have seen no sport, so now I will go abroad to seek adventure. Stay here in the greenwood and listen for my call. Three blasts upon the bugle horn I will blow in my hour of need. Then come quickly, for I shall want your aid."

Robin strode away through the leafy forest glades until he had come to the verge of Sherwood. At last he took a road by the forest skirts, a bypath that dipped toward a broad, pebbly stream spanned by a narrow bridge made of a log. As he drew near this bridge he saw a tall stranger coming from the other side. Then Robin walked quicker, as did the stranger, each thinking to cross first.

"Stand back," said Robin, "and let the better man cross first."

"Stand back yourself," answered the stranger, "for I am the better man."

"We will see," said Robin. "Meanwhile, stand where you are, or I will send an arrow between your ribs."

"You speak like a coward," answered the stranger, "for you stand there with a bow to shoot at my heart, while I have nothing but a plain blackthorn staff."

"I have never had a coward's name in all my life," said Robin. "I will put down my bow and arrows, and cut a staff to fight you."

Robin Hood cut a good staff of oak, six feet in length, and came back trimming away the tender stems from it, while the stranger waited for him, leaning upon his staff and whistling as he gazed round about. Robin had never seen a stouter man. Tall was Robin, but taller was the stranger by a head and a neck, for he was seven feet in height. Broad was Robin across the shoulders, but the stranger was even broader across shoulder and waist.

"Here is my good staff," Robin cried. "Now wait my coming, if you dare, and we will fight until one of us tumbles into the stream."

In response, the stranger twirled his staff above his head until it whistled.

Never did the knights of Arthur's Round Table meet in a bolder fight than did these two. Robin stepped quickly upon the bridge where the stranger stood. He delivered a blow at the stranger's head that would have tumbled him into the water, had it met its mark. But the stranger turned the blow away and in return gave one just as strong, which Robin also turned away, as the stranger had done.

So they stood, each in his place, for one good hour, and many blows were given and received by each in that time, till both had sore bones and bumps, yet neither thought of crying "Enough!" nor seemed likely to fall off the bridge. Now and then they stopped to rest, and each thought that he never had seen in all his life such skill at the quarterstaff.

At last Robin gave the stranger a blow upon the ribs that made his jacket smoke like a damp straw thatch in the sun. The stranger came within a hair's breadth of falling off the bridge, but he regained himself quickly. With a dexterous blow he sent Robin heels over head into the water.

"Where are you now, my good lad?" shouted the stranger, roaring with laughter.

"Floating away with the tide," cried Robin, for he could not help laughing at what had happened. Then he waded to the bank. "Give me your hand," he called. "I must admit you are brave and skilled with the staff. My head hums like a hive of bees on a hot June day."

He clapped his horn to his lips and blew a blast that echoed down the forest paths. "I say again, you are a tall lad, and a brave one. There is no man who could do to me what you have done."

"And you," said the stranger, laughing, "take your beating like a brave man."

Now the distant twigs and branches rustled with the coming of men, and suddenly twenty or more stout yeomen, all clad in Lincoln green, burst out, with merry Will Stutely at their head.

"Good master," cried Will, "how is this? You are wet from head to foot."

"This stout fellow has tumbled me into the water and given me a beating besides," Robin explained.

"Then he shall not go without a ducking and a beating himself!" cried Will Stutely. "Have at him, lads!"

Will and a score of yeomen leaped upon the stranger, but though they sprang quickly, they found him ready and felt him strike right and left with his stout staff.

"No, stop!" cried Robin, laughing until his sore sides ached again. "He is a fine man and true, and no harm shall befall him. Good man, will you stay with me and be one of my band? You shall share with us whatever good shall befall us and be my right-hand man. Will you be one of my merry men?"

"Yes, I will, for now and for always."

"Then I have gained a good man this day," said Robin. "What is your name, good fellow?"

"John Little," answered the stranger.

Then Will Stutely, who loved a good jest, said, "No, that name does not fit you. We will call you Little John."

"That name fits you well," said Robin Hood. "Little John shall you be called from now on." And so Little John joined Robin's merry band.

The Shooting Match at Nottingham Town

IT CAME TO the Sheriff of Nottingham's ears that the people laughed at him for not being able to capture Robin, the bold outlaw. "Now," thought the Sheriff, "if I could just persuade Robin to come to Nottingham Town, I would lay hands upon him so that he would never get away again." It suddenly occurred to the Sheriff that were he to proclaim a great shooting match and offer some grand prize, Robin Hood might be tempted to come.

So the Sheriff sent messengers north and south, and east and west, to proclaim through town, hamlet, and countryside this grand shooting match, and every-one was invited who could draw a longbow, and the prize was to be an arrow of pure gold.

When Robin Hood heard the news, he called his merry men about him. “Listen,” he told them. “Our friend the Sheriff of Nottingham has proclaimed a shooting match, and the prize is to be a bright golden arrow. I would like one of us to win it, both because of the fairness of the prize and because our friend the Sheriff has offered it.”

Young David of Doncaster said, “I have heard more news about this match. The Sheriff has done this to lay a trap for you. He wishes nothing more than to see you there so he can capture you. Please do not go, good master.”

“You are a wise lad,” said Robin. “But shall we let it be said that the Sheriff of Nottingham frightened bold Robin Hood and the best archers in England? What you tell me makes me desire the prize even more. But we must meet trickery with trickery. Some of you clothe yourselves as friars, and some as peasants, and some as beggars, but see that each man takes a good bow or broadsword in case they are needed. As for myself, I will shoot for this same golden arrow, and should I win it, we will hang it to the branches of our greenwood tree for the joy of all the band."

A fair sight was Nottingham Town on the day of the shooting match. All along the green meadow beneath the town wall stretched a row of benches, which were for knights and ladies and rich merchants and their wives. At the end of the range, near the target, was a raised seat bedecked with ribbons and garlands of flowers, for the Sheriff of Nottingham and his lady.

Across the range from the seats for the better folk was a railing to keep the poorer people from crowding in front of the target. Already the benches were beginning to fill with people of quality. With these came also the poorer folk, who sat or lay upon the green grass near the railing that kept them off the range. In the great tent, the archers were gathering by twos and threes. And never was such a company of yeomen as were gathered at Nottingham Town that day, for the best archers of England had come to this shooting match.

At last the Sheriff himself came with his lady. When the Sheriff and his lady had sat down, his herald blew his silver horn. The archers stepped forward to their places, while all the spectators shouted with a mighty voice, each man calling upon his favorite to do his best.

The Sheriff leaned forward, looking keenly among the press of archers to find whether Robin Hood was among them. But none was clad in Lincoln green, the color worn by Robin and his band. "Nevertheless," said the Sheriff to himself, "he may still be here, and I have missed him among the crowd. Let me see the best men shoot, for I wager he will be among them."

Now the archers began shooting, each man in turn, and the good folk never saw such archery as was done that day. Finally, only ten men were left in the competition. Of these ten, six were famous throughout the land. Two others were from Yorkshire; another was a tall stranger in blue, who said he came from London Town; and the last was a tattered stranger in scarlet, who wore a patch over one eye.

"Now," said the Sheriff to a man-at-arms nearby, "do you see Robin Hood among those ten?"

"No, I do not, Your Worship," answered the man. "Six of them I know well. Of the others, one is too tall and the other too short. Robin's beard is as yellow as gold, while that tattered beggar in scarlet has a beard of brown, besides being blind in one eye. As for the stranger in blue, Robin's shoulders are three inches broader than his."

"Then," said the Sheriff angrily, "Robin Hood is a coward as well as a rogue, and dares not show his face among good men."

After they had rested a short time, the ten men stepped forth to shoot again. Each man shot two arrows, and the crowd watched with scarcely a sound. When the last had shot his arrow, another great shout arose, while many cast their caps aloft for joy of such marvelous shooting.

Now only three men were left. One was Gilbert o' the Red Cap, one the tattered stranger in scarlet, and one Adam o' the Dell of Tamworth. The spectators called aloud, some crying, "Ho for Gilbert o' the Red Cap!"

and some, "Hey for stout Adam o' the Dell!" But not a single man in the crowd called upon the stranger in scarlet.

Gilbert was the first to shoot. His arrow flew straight and hit the target a finger's breadth from the center. "Now, that is a great shot!" cried the Sheriff.

Then the tattered stranger stepped forth, and everyone laughed as they saw a yellow patch beneath his arm when he raised his elbow to shoot, and also to see him aim with only one eye. He drew the yew bow and shot an arrow so quickly that no man could take a breath between the drawing and the shooting. His arrow lodged nearer the center than the other. "Now that was a lovely shot, in truth!" cried the Sheriff.

Then Adam o' the Dell shot, carefully and cautiously, and his arrow lodged close beside the stranger's. Then they all three shot again. This time Adam o' the Dell's was farthest from the center, and again the tattered stranger's shot was the best.

Then they all shot for the third time. This time Gilbert took great care to aim. Straight flew his arrow, and the shaft lodged close beside the spot that marked the very center.

"Well done, Gilbert!" cried the Sheriff. "I believe the prize is yours. Now, you ragged knave, let me see you shoot a better shaft than that."

The stranger said nothing but took his place, while no one spoke or even seemed to breathe, so great was the silence for wonder of how he would do. Then straight flew the arrow, and so true that it smote a gray goose feather from off Gilbert's shaft, which fell fluttering through the sunlit air as the stranger's arrow lodged close beside his and in the very center. No one spoke a word for a while and no one shouted, but each man looked into his neighbor's face with amazement.

The Sheriff came down and drew near to where the tattered stranger stood leaning upon his stout bow, while the good folk crowded around to see the man who shot so well. "Here, good fellow," said the Sheriff, "take the prize, and well and fairly have you won it. I wager you are a better man than that coward Robin Hood, who dared not show his face here this day. Say, good fellow, will you join my service?"

"No, I will not," said the stranger roughly. "No man in all England shall be my master."

"Then get away from here, before I beat you for your disrespectful tongue," shouted the Sheriff. He turned and strode away.

It was a merry company that gathered about the noble greenwood tree in Sherwood's depths that day. Some barefoot friars were there, and some men that looked like beggars. Seated upon a mossy couch was one all clad in tattered scarlet, with a patch over one eye. In his hand he held the golden arrow that was the prize of the great shooting match. Amid the talking and laughter, he took the patch from his eye, stripped off his scarlet rags, and washed the walnut dye from his yellow hair. Then all laughed louder than before, for it was Robin Hood himself who had won the prize from the Sheriff's hands.

All sat down to the woodland feast and talked of the merry joke that had been played upon the Sheriff, and of the adventures that had befallen each member of the band in disguise.

But when the feast was done, Robin Hood took Little John aside and said, "Truly am I angry, for today I heard the Sheriff call Robin Hood a coward who dared not show his face. I would like to let him know who won the golden arrow from his hand, and also that I am no coward."

Little John said, “Good master, Will Stutely and I will go and send the Sheriff news of all this by a messenger he does not expect.”

That day the Sheriff sat at dinner in the great hall of his house at Nottingham Town. Long tables lined the hall, filled with men-at-arms and household servants. There they talked of the day’s shooting as they ate their meal.

“I did think that Robin Hood would be at the game today,” said the Sheriff. “I did not think he was such a coward.”

Then, even as he finished speaking, something fell rattling among the dishes on the table. One of the men-at-arms picked it up and brought it to the Sheriff. Everyone saw that it was a blunted gray goose shaft, with a fine scroll tied near its head. The Sheriff opened the scroll and glanced at it, while the veins upon his forehead swelled and his cheeks grew ruddy with rage as he read, for this is what he saw:

"Now Heaven bless Thy Grace this day
Say all in sweet Sherwood
For you did give the prize away
To merry Robin Hood."

Will Stutely Rescued by His Companions

WHEN THE SHERIFF found that neither law nor trickery could overcome Robin Hood, he was perplexed. The Sheriff said to himself, "I am a fool! Had I not told King Henry about Robin Hood, I would not have gotten myself into such a predicament. But now I must either take him captive or have his most gracious Majesty rain anger on my head. I have tried law, and I have tried trickery, and I have failed in both; so I will try what may be done with might."

The Sheriff called his best yeomen together and told them what he had in mind. "Each of you take four men, all armed," said he, "and go to Sherwood Forest. Hide yourselves in different places and lie in wait for that outlaw, Robin Hood. If any of you finds too many men against him, let him sound a horn, and then let each band within hearing come with all speed and join the group that called them.

"In this way, we shall take the green-clad knave. Furthermore, to him that first meets Robin Hood I will give one hundred pounds of silver if he be brought to me dead or alive. And to anyone who meets with any of his band I shall give forty pounds if such be brought to me dead or alive. So, I tell all of you, be bold and be crafty."

So they went in sixty companies of five into Sherwood Forest to take Robin Hood, each constable wishing that he might be the one to find the bold outlaw, or at least one of his band. For seven days and nights they hunted through the forest glades, but never saw so much as a single man in Lincoln green. For news of the Sheriff's plan had been brought to Robin Hood by trusty Eadom, landlord of the Sign of the Blue Boar.

When he first heard the news, Robin said, "If the Sheriff dares to send force to meet force, woe will it be for him and his men, for blood will flow and there will be great trouble for all. But I would rather not take part in a bloody battle, nor do I want to deal sorrow to the families and wives of good yeomen who lose their lives. So now we will abide silently in Sherwood Forest, so that it may be well for all, but should we be forced to defend ourselves, or any of our band, then let each man draw a bow and use it with all his skill."

At this speech many of the band shook their heads and said to themselves, "Now the Sheriff will think that we are cowards, and folk will laugh at us throughout the countryside, saying that we fear to meet these men." But they said nothing aloud, swallowing their words and doing as Robin told them.

Thus they hid in the depths of Sherwood Forest for seven days and seven nights and never showed their faces abroad. But early in the morning of the eighth day, Robin Hood called the band together and said, "Who will go and find what the Sheriff's men are doing? I know they will not stay forever within Sherwood's glades."

At this a great shout arose, and each man waved his bow aloft and cried that he might be the one to go. Robin Hood's heart was proud when he looked around on his stout, brave fellows, and he said, "Brave and true are you all, my merry men, and a right stout band of good fellows you are, but all of you cannot go. So I will choose one from among you, and it shall be good Will Stutely, for he is as sly as the foxes that live in Sherwood Forest."

Will Stutely jumped up, clapping his hands for joy that he had been chosen. "Thanks, good master," he said, "and trust that I will bring you news of the Sheriff's men, or my name is not Will Stutely."

He dressed himself in a friar's gown, and underneath the robe he hung a good broadsword that he could easily lay his hands on. He set forth upon his quest, until he came to the highway. There he saw two bands of the Sheriff's men, yet he turned neither to the right nor the left, but only drew his hood closer over his face and folded his hands in front of him. At last he came to the Sign of the Blue Boar. "Our good friend Eadom will tell me all the news," he said to himself.

At the Sign of the Blue Boar he found a band of the Sheriff's men eating and drinking heartily. Without speaking to anyone, he sat down upon a bench, his staff in his hand, and his head bowed as though he were meditating. Thus he sat waiting until he might see the landlord alone. But Eadom did not know him, only thinking he was some poor, tired friar, so he let him sit without saying a word to him or bothering him.

As Stutely sat, a large house cat came and rubbed against his knee, raising his robe a palm's breadth high. Stutely pushed his robe quickly down again, but the constable who commanded the Sheriff's men saw what had happened, and saw also fair Lincoln green beneath the friar's robe. He said nothing at the time, but told himself, "That is no friar, and also, no honest yeoman goes about in a priest's clothing. I think that is one of Robin Hood's men."

The constable said aloud, "Oh, holy father, will you not take a bottle to quench your thirsty soul?"

Stutely shook his head silently, saying to himself, "Maybe someone here knows my voice."

The constable said, "Where do you go, holy father, upon this hot summer's day?"

"I go as a pilgrim to Canterbury Town," answered Will Stutely, speaking gruffly, so no one might recognize his voice.

The constable spoke for the third time, "Tell me, holy father, do pilgrims to Canterbury wear good Lincoln green beneath their robes? Ha! I believe you are a thief, and perhaps one of Robin Hood's band! By Our Lady's grace, if you move your hand or your foot, I will run through your body with my sword!"

The constable flashed his bright sword and leaped upon Will Stutely, thinking he would take him off guard. But Stutely held his own sword tightly beneath his robe, so he drew it forth before the constable came upon him. The constable struck a mighty blow, but Stutely skillfully parried the blow and struck the constable back with all his might. Stutely would have escaped, but he could not, for the other man, dizzy from the blow and his flowing blood, seized him by the knees even as he reeled and fell. The others rushed upon him. Stutely struck again at another of the Sheriff's men, but his steel cap deflected the blow, and though the blade bit deep, it did not kill.

Meanwhile, the constable, even though he was fainting from loss of blood, dragged Stutely downward, and the others, seeing the yeoman struggling to free himself, rushed upon him again. One man struck a blow upon Will's head so that the blood ran down his face and blinded him. Staggering, Will fell, and all sprang upon him, though he struggled so manfully that they could hardly hold him down. Finally, they bound him with stout rope so he could not move hand or foot, and thus they overcame him.

* * *

Robin Hood stood under the greenwood tree, thinking of Will Stutely and how he might be faring, when suddenly he saw two of his merry men come running down the forest path, and between them ran Maken, a maid at the Blue Boar. Robin's heart fell, for he knew they were bringing bad news.

"Will Stutely has been taken," Maken cried. "I saw it all, and I fear he is badly hurt, for one struck him mightily in the head. They have bound him and taken him to Nottingham Town, and before I left the Blue Boar I heard that he will be hanged tomorrow afternoon."

"He shall not be hanged tomorrow afternoon," cried Robin. "Or if he is, many other men shall lose their lives that day, and there will be much crying and wailing in sorrow."

Robin clapped his horn to his lips and blew three loud blasts. His good yeomen came running through the greenwood until one hundred forty men were gathered around him.

"Now all of you, listen!" cried Robin. "Our dear companion Will Stutely has been taken by that vile Sheriff's men. We must take bow and staff to bring him home again. We must risk life and limb for him, as he has risked life and limb for us. Is it not so, my merry men?" All cried "Ay!" with a great voice.

The next day they made their way from Sherwood Forest, but by different paths. The band separated into parties of twos and threes, which were all to meet again in a tangled wood that lay near Nottingham Town. Then, when they had all gathered together at the place of meeting, Robin spoke to them, saying:

"We will lie here in ambush until we can get news, for it is best to be cunning and wary if we would bring our friend Will Stutely back from the Sheriff's clutches."

They lay hidden a long time, until the sun stood high in the sky. The day was warm and the dusty roads were bare of travelers, except an old man who walked slowly along the highroad that led near the gray castle wall of Nottingham Town. When Robin saw that no other traveler was in sight, he called young David of Doncaster, who was a clever man, and said to him, "Now, young David, go out and speak to that man who walks beside the town wall, for he has come just now from Nottingham Town and may tell you news of good Stutely."

David strode forth, and when he came up to the man, he saluted him and said, "Fine day, good sir. Can you tell me when Will Stutely will be hanged upon the gallows tree? I would not miss the sight, for I have come from far away to see so sturdy a rogue hanged."

"Get away from me, young man," cried the elder, "and shame on you for speaking so eagerly when a good man is to be hanged for nothing but guarding his own life!" He struck his staff upon the ground in anger. "It is a terrible thing that he is to be hanged this day, toward evening, when the sun falls low, near the great town gate of Nottingham, where three roads meet. For there the Sheriff has decreed he shall die as a warning to all outlaws in Nottinghamshire.

"But yet, I say again, it is a sorrowful thing. Alas! For though Robin Hood and his band may be outlaws, they take only from the rich and the dishonest men, while there is not a poor widow nor a peasant with many children near Sherwood who hasn't enough flour to last all year long because of him. My heart is heavy to see one as gallant as Will Stutely die, for I was a good yeoman in my day, and I love a strong hand that strikes at a cruel lord with fat moneybags. If only good Stutely's master knew how much trouble his man was in, perhaps he might send some aid to bring him out of the grip of his enemies."

"Yes, that is certainly true," cried David of Doncaster. "If Robin and his men are near this place, I am sure they will try to bring him out of danger. Fare you well, my good man, and believe me, if Will Stutely should die, Robin Hood will have his revenge."

He turned and hurried away, but the old man looked after him, muttering, "I think that youth is no country lad who has come to see a good man die. Well, well, maybe Robin Hood is not so far away but that there will be bold doings this day." So he went on his way.

When David of Doncaster told Robin Hood all the old man had said to him, Robin called the band around him and spoke to them.

"Let us get quickly into Nottingham Town and mix with the people there. Keep one another in sight, pressing as near the prisoner and his guards as you can when they come outside the walls. Strike no man without need, for I would avoid bloodshed, but if you do strike, strike hard, and see that there be no need to strike again. Let us keep all together until we come again to Sherwood, and let no man leave his fellows behind."

The sun was low in the western sky when a bugle note sounded from the castle wall. Then crowds filled the streets of Nottingham Town, for all knew that the famous Will Stutely was to be hanged that day. The castle gates opened wide and a great array of men-at-arms came forth with noise and clatter, the Sheriff, all clad in shining armor, riding at their head. In the midst of all, in a cart, with a halter about his neck, rode Will Stutely. His face was pale from his wound and loss of blood, and his fair hair was clotted where the blood had hardened. When he came forth from the castle, he looked up and down, but though he saw some faces that showed pity and some that showed friendliness, he saw none he knew. His heart sank, but he spoke up boldly.

"Give a sword into my hand, Sir Sheriff," said he, "and wounded though I be, I will fight you and all your men until my life and strength be gone."

"No," said the Sheriff, turning his head and looking grimly at Will Stutely. "You shall have no sword. You shall die a coward's death as is fitting for the vile thief you are."

"Then at least untie my hands, and I will fight you and your men with no weapon besides my bare fists," Will cried. "I need no weapon, but let me not be hanged this day."

The Sheriff laughed. "Why, what's wrong?" he said. "Are you afraid to die? Say your prayers, you vile knave, for I intend to hang you this day where the three roads meet, so that all men shall see you hang, and for the crows to peck at your body."

"Then listen to my words," cried Will Stutely. "If ever my good master should meet you, you will pay dearly for this day's work! He hates you, and so do all brave hearts. Don't you know that your name is a joke on the lips of every brave man in Nottinghamshire? Someone like you will never be able to capture bold Robin Hood."

"What?" cried the Sheriff in a rage. "You say I am a joke with your master, as you call him? Now I will make a joke of you, and a sorry joke it will be, for I will cut you limb from limb after you are hanged." He spurred his horse forward and said no more to Stutely.

At last they came to the great town gate, through which Stutely saw the fair country beyond, with hills and dales all clothed in green, and far away the dusky line of Sherwood Forest. When he saw the slanting sunlight lying on the fields, there came a great heaviness to his heart. He bowed his head so that people would not think him a coward when they saw tears in his eyes. Thus he kept his head bowed till they had passed through the gate and were outside the walls of the town.

But when Will looked up again, he felt his heart leap within him and then stand still for joy, for he saw the face of one of his own dear companions of merry Sherwood. Glancing quickly around, he saw familiar faces upon all sides, crowding closely upon the men-at-arms who were guarding him. The blood sprang to his cheeks, for he saw his own good master in the crowd. Then Will knew that Robin Hood and his band were there. Yet between him and them was a line of men-at-arms.

"Stand back!" cried the Sheriff in a mighty voice, for the crowd pressed around on all sides. "What do you mean by pushing against us? Stand back, I say!"

Then came a bustle and a noise. One man tried to push between the men-at-arms to reach the cart, and Stutely saw it was Little John who made the commotion.

"Stand back!" cried one of the men-at-arms whom Little John pushed.

"Stand back, yourself," said Little John, and struck the man a blow that felled him as a butcher fells an ox. Little John leaped to the cart where Stutely sat.

"I hope you will say good-bye to your friends before you die, Will," said Little John. "Or maybe I will die with you if you must die, for I could never have better company." With one stroke Little John cut the ropes that bound the other's arms and legs, and Stutely leaped out of the cart.

"Now as I live," cried the Sheriff, "I know that rebel! He is one of Robin Hood's men. Take him, I bid you all, and do not let him go!"

He spurred his horse upon Little John, and rising in his stirrups struck with all his strength, but Little John ducked underneath the horse's belly and the blow whistled harmlessly over his head.

"No, good Sir Sheriff," cried Little John, leaping up again, "I must borrow your trusty sword." He twisted the weapon from the Sheriff's hand. "Here, Stutely," he cried, "the Sheriff has lent you his sword! Stand back-to-back with me, man, and defend yourself, for help is near!"

"Down with them!" bellowed the Sheriff. He spurred his horse upon the two who now stood back-to-back, forgetting in his rage that he had no weapon to defend himself.

"Stand back, Sheriff!" cried Little John. A bugle horn sounded shrilly and an arrow whistled within an inch of the Sheriff's head. Then came much shouting and swearing, cries and groans and clashing of steel. Swords flashed in the setting sun, and a score of arrows whistled through the air. Some people cried, "Help, help!" and some, "A rescue, a rescue!"

"Treason!" cried the Sheriff. "Get back! Get back or else we will all be dead men!" He reined his horse backward through the thickest of the crowd and was gone.

Robin Hood and his band might have slain half of the Sheriff's men had they wanted to, but they let them run away, although they did send a bunch of arrows after them to hurry them in their flight.

"Stay!" shouted Will Stutely after the Sheriff. "You will never catch bold Robin Hood if you do not stand to meet him face-to-face." But the Sheriff, crouched low along his horse's back, made no answer, but only spurred his mount to escape faster.

Will Stutely turned to Little John and looked at him till tears ran from his eyes and he wept aloud. "Oh, Little John!" he cried. "My own true friend, whom I love better than anyone in all the world! I did not think to see your face this day." Little John could not answer, but wept also.

Robin Hood gathered his band together, with Will Stutely in the middle, and they moved away toward Sherwood, and were gone. But they left ten of the Sheriff's men lying on the ground wounded—some more, some less—yet no one knew who struck them down.

Thus the Sheriff of Nottingham tried more than once to take Robin Hood and failed each time. This last time he was frightened, for he felt how near he had come to losing his life. So he said, "These men fear neither God nor man, nor king nor king's officers. I would sooner lose

my office than my life, so I will trouble them no more."
He stayed within his castle for many a day and dared not show his face outside of his own household, and all the time he was gloomy and would speak to no one, for he was ashamed of what had happened that day.

The Sheriff Comes to Sherwood Forest

AFTER ALL THESE THINGS had happened, and Robin Hood learned how the Sheriff had tried to make him captive, he said to himself, "If I have the chance, I will make our Sheriff pay for what he has done. Maybe I will bring him into Sherwood Forest and have him as a guest at a merry feast with us." For when Robin Hood caught a baron or a squire or a bishop, he brought them to the greenwood tree and fed them before he lightened their purses.

One day Robin set forth to seek adventure, strolling along until he came to the edge of Sherwood. There he met a young butcher on his way to market, driving a fine mare and riding in a new cart, stocked with meat.

"Good morning," said Robin. "Where are you going?"

"I go to the market at Nottingham Town to sell my beef and my mutton," answered the butcher.

"Pray, tell me for what price you will sell me all of your meat and your horse and cart."

"Four marks," said the butcher.

Robin Hood plucked out his purse and said, "Here in this purse are six marks. I would like to be a butcher for the day and sell my meat in Nottingham Town. Will you close a bargain with me and take six marks for all?"

The butcher was joyful at this bargain. He leaped down from his cart and took the purse that Robin held out to him.

Robin put on the butcher's apron and, climbing into the cart, took the reins and drove off through the forest to Nottingham Town.

When Robin came to Nottingham, he entered that part of the market where butchers stood, and set up his cart in the best place he could find. Next, he opened his stall and spread his meat upon the bench; then, taking his cleaver and steel and clattering them together, he shouted, "Now, who will buy? Four fixed prices have I. Three penny-worths of meat I sell to a lord or priest for sixpence, for I don't want their business. Merchants I charge nothing, for I like their business the best of all."

All began to stare and wonder and crowd around, laughing, for never was such selling heard of in Nottingham Town. But when they came to buy they found it as he had said. Many came to his stall, and Robin sold his meat so fast that no butcher near him could sell anything.

Then some of the butchers came to meet him. "Come, brother," said one who was the head of them all, "we are all in the same trade. Will you dine with us? For this day the Sheriff has asked all the Butcher Guild to feast with him at the guildhall."

Robin agreed and went with them to the great guildhall. When he and those that were with him came in, all laughing at some merry jest he had been telling them, those that were near the Sheriff whispered to him, "That mad butcher has sold more meat for one penny this day than we could sell for three. He must have sold his land for silver and gold, and means to spend his money."

The Sheriff called Robin to him, not knowing him in his butcher's clothing, and made him sit close to him on his right hand. For he loved a rich young man, especially when he thought that he might empty that youth's pockets into his own purse. So he made much of Robin, and laughed and talked with him more than with any of the others.

"You are a right merry soul," said the Sheriff, "and you must have many herds of horned beasts and many an acre of land, that you spend your money so freely."

"Yes, I have," said Robin, laughing again. "Five hundred and more horned beasts have I and my brothers, but we have never been able to sell them. As for my land, I have never asked my steward how many acres I have."

At this the Sheriff's eyes twinkled, and he chuckled to himself. "If you cannot sell your horned beasts, maybe I will buy them from you. How much do you want?"

"Well," said Robin, "they are worth at least five hundred pounds."

"No," answered the Sheriff slowly, and as if he were thinking, "I will give you three hundred pounds for them all, and that in good hard silver and gold."

"Well, you know that so many horned beasts are worth seven hundred pounds and more," Robin cried. "But I will take your offer, for I and my brothers do need the money. Be sure you bring three hundred pounds with you to close the bargain."

"I will bring the money," said the Sheriff. "But what is your name, good youth?"

"Men call me Robert o' Locksley," said bold Robin.

"Then, good Robert o' Locksley," said the Sheriff, "I will come this day to see your fine beasts."

That afternoon the Sheriff mounted his horse and joined Robin Hood, who stood outside the gateway of the paved court waiting for him, for he had sold his horse and cart to a trader for two marks. Then they set out on their way, the Sheriff riding upon his horse and Robin running beside him. Thus they left Nottingham Town and traveled along the dusty highway, laughing and jesting together as though they were old friends. But all the time the Sheriff said to himself, "Your bargain shall cost you plenty, you fool."

So they journeyed till they came near Sherwood Forest. The Sheriff looked up and down and to the right and to the left, and then grew quiet and ceased his laughter. "Now," said he, "may Heaven and its saints preserve us this day from a rogue whom men call Robin Hood."

Robin laughed aloud. "Nay," said he, "you may set your mind at rest, for well do I know Robin Hood and well do I know that you are in no more danger from him this day than you are from me."

At last they came to where the road took a sudden bend, and before them a herd of deer ran across the path. Robin Hood came close to the Sheriff, and pointing his finger, he said, "These are my horned beasts, good Master Sheriff. How do you like them?"

The Sheriff drew his rein quickly. "Now, fellow," said he, "I wish I were out of this forest, for I do not like your company. Go your own path, good friend, and let me go mine."

But Robin only laughed and caught the Sheriff's bridle rein. "No," cried he, "stay awhile, for I would like you to see my brothers, who own these fair horned beasts with me." So saying, he clapped his bugle to his mouth and blew three merry notes. Soon a hundred yeomen with Little John at their head came up the path.

"What do you wish, good master?" said Little John.

"I have brought company to feast with us today," answered Robin. "It is our good master, the Sheriff of Nottingham. Take his bridle, Little John, for he has honored us today by coming to feast with us."

So Little John took the bridle rein and led the horse deeper into the forest, all marching in order, with Robin Hood walking beside the Sheriff, hat in hand.

All this time the Sheriff said never a word but only looked about him like one suddenly awakened from sleep. When he found himself going into the depths of Sherwood his heart sank, for he thought, "Surely my three hundred pounds will be taken from me, even if they take not my life itself, for I have plotted against their lives more than once." But everyone seemed humble and meek and not a word was said of danger, either to life or money.

At last they came to that part of Sherwood Forest where a noble oak spread its branches wide, and beneath it was a seat of moss, on which Robin sat down, placing the Sheriff at his right hand. "Bring out the best we have, for the Sheriff has feasted me in Nottingham guildhall today, and I would not have him go back hungry," Robin commanded.

All this time nothing had been said of the Sheriff's money, so he began to take heart. "For," said the Sheriff to himself, "maybe Robin Hood has forgotten all about it."

Robin Hood provided entertainment for the Sheriff. First, several men battled with quarterstaffs, and so quickly did they parry that the Sheriff clapped his hands, forgetting where he was, and cried aloud, "Well struck!"

Then several yeomen came forward and spread cloths upon the green grass, and placed a royal feast. Then all sat down and feasted merrily together until the sun was low.

The Sheriff rose and said, "I thank you all for the merry entertainment you have given me this day. But the shadows grow long, and I must be on my way before darkness comes."

Robin Hood and all his merry men arose also, and Robin said to the Sheriff, "Go if you must, but you have forgotten one thing. We keep a merry inn here in the greenwood, but whoever becomes our guest must pay his reckoning. I would not dishonor the Sheriff by saying this feast was worth any less than three hundred pounds. Is it not so, my merry men?"

"Three hundred pounds!" roared the Sheriff. "I would not give you *three* pounds for such a poor feast!"

"There be those here who do not love you as much as I do," said Robin gravely. "Good Sheriff, I advise you to pay without any trouble, or it may not go well for you."

The Sheriff looked around at Robin's men and saw they were glaring at him in anger, their quarterstaffs at the ready. Slowly he drew forth his fat purse and threw it upon the cloth in front of him.

"Now take the purse, Little John," said Robin Hood, "and see that the reckoning is right."

Little John counted the money and found that the bag held three hundred pounds in silver and gold. To the Sheriff it seemed as if every clink of the bright money were a drop of blood from his veins. When he saw it all counted out in a heap of silver and gold, filling a wooden platter, he turned away and silently mounted his horse.

"Never have we had so important a guest before!" said Robin. "Because the day grows late, I will lead you out of the forest myself." Taking the Sheriff's horse by the bridle rein, Robin led him to the main forest path.

Then bitterly did the Sheriff regret the day that first he meddled with Robin Hood, for all men laughed at him, and many ballads were sung by folk throughout the country of how the Sheriff went to shear and came home shorn himself. For thus men sometimes overreach through greed and guile.

Robin Hood Shoots before Queen Eleanor

ONE HOT SUMMER afternoon, a youth came riding along the road to Sherwood Forest. His long yellow hair flowed as he rode along, all clad in silk and velvet, with jewels flashing and dagger jingling against the pommel of the saddle. Thus came the queen's page, young Richard Partington, from famous London Town into Nottinghamshire, upon Her Majesty's bidding, to seek Robin Hood in Sherwood Forest.

The road was hot and dusty and his journey had been long, so young Partington was glad when he saw before him a sweet little inn, all shady and cool beneath the trees. As he sat drinking, five yeomen watched him. Two were clothed in Lincoln green, and a great heavy oaken staff leaned against the gnarled oak tree trunk beside each fellow.

Partington saw the men watching him and raised his glass in a toast. "Here is to the health and long happiness of my royal mistress, the noble Queen Eleanor. May my journey and her wish soon end, and I find a certain man called Robin Hood."

At these words the two men in Lincoln green began whispering together. One of them asked, "Why do you seek Robin Hood, Sir Page? And what does our good Queen Eleanor wish of him? I ask you for good reason, for I may know this Robin Hood."

"If you know him, you will do great service to him and great pleasure to our royal queen by helping me find him. I bring a kind message to him from our queen."

The two yeomen spoke together. Both arose, and the tall yeoman said, "We think your words are true, Sir Page, and mean no harm, so we will guide you to Robin Hood as you wish."

In the cool shade under the greenwood tree, Robin Hood and many of his band lay upon the grass. Soon Little John and Will Stutely came forth from the forest, with young Richard Partington riding between them. Robin arose and stepped forth to meet him. Partington leaped from his horse and met Robin as he came. "Welcome!" cried Robin. "Tell me what brings one so fair and wearing such noble garb to our poor forest of Sherwood?"

Young Partington said, "I bring greetings from our noble Queen Eleanor. Many times has she heard of you and your merry deeds. She would like to meet you. Therefore she sent me to bring you to London Town.

She will guard you against harm, and will send you back safely to Sherwood Forest again. Four days from now, in Finsbury Fields, our good King Henry will hold a grand shooting match, and all the most famous archers of merry England will be there. Our queen would like to see you compete and, no doubt, carry off the prize. She sends to you, as a sign of great goodwill, this golden ring from her own fair thumb."

Robin Hood bowed and, taking the ring, kissed it loyally, then slipped it upon his little finger. He said, "I will do our queen's bidding and will go with thee to London."

Robin chose Little John, Will Scarlet, and Allan a Dale to go with him, and soon all five departed upon their way.

Four days they traveled, till they came at last to the towers and walls of famous London Town, while the morning was still young and golden toward the east.

Queen Eleanor sat in her royal tower, when a messenger said that her page, Richard Partington, and four stout yeomen waited for her in the court below. Queen Eleanor arose joyously and ordered them to be shown into her presence.

Robin Hood, Little John, Will Scarlet, and Allan a Dale came before the queen. Robin knelt before the queen with his hands folded upon his chest, saying, "Here am I, Robin Hood. You bid me come, and lo, I do your bidding. I give myself to you as your true servant, and will do anything you command, even if it means I shed the last drop of my life's blood."

Good Queen Eleanor smiled pleasantly upon him, bidding him to rise. She made them all be seated to rest themselves after their long journey. Rich food and drink were brought in, and they spoke of Robin Hood's many adventures. So the time passed till the hour drew nigh for the great archery match in Finsbury Fields.

A merry sight were the famous Finsbury Fields on that sunny morning. Along the end of the meadow stood the booths for the bands of archers. On each side of the archery range were rows upon rows of seats reaching high above, and in the center of the north side was a raised dais for the king and queen, shaded by canvas of bright colors and hung about with streaming silken pennants of red and blue and green and white.

As yet, the king and queen had not arrived, but the other benches were full of people. One hundred sixty yards from the mark from which the archers were to shoot stood ten targets. All was ready for the coming of the king and queen.

At last a great blast of bugles sounded, and into the meadow came riding six trumpeters with silver trumpets, from which hung velvet banners heavy with silver and gold thread. Behind these came stout King Henry upon a gray stallion, with his queen beside him upon a milk-white pony. On either side of them walked the yeomen of the guard, the bright sunlight flashing from the polished blades of their steel halberds. Behind these came the court in a great crowd, so that soon all the lawn was alive with bright colors, with waving plumes and gleaming gold.

All the people arose and shouted, so that their voices sounded like a storm upon the coast. The king and queen came to their place, and getting down from their horses, they mounted the broad stairs that led to the raised platform, where they took their seats on two thrones bedecked with purple silks and cloths of silver and of gold.

When all was quiet a bugle sounded, and the archers came marching from their tents. Eighty they were in all, as stalwart a band of yeomen as could be found in all the world. So they came in orderly fashion and stood in front of the dais where King Henry and his queen sat. King Henry looked up and down their ranks, for his heart warmed at the sight of such a gallant band of yeomen. Then he bade his herald, Sir Hugh de Mowbray, to stand and proclaim the rules governing the match.

After Sir Hugh had spoken, each band turned and marched back to its place. Then the shooting began, the captains first speeding their shafts and then making room for the men who shot, each in turn, after them. Two hundred and eighty shafts were shot in all, and so deftly were they sped that when the shooting was done each target looked like the back of a hedgehog. When it was over the judges came forward, looked carefully at the targets, and proclaimed which three had shot the best from the separate bands. Then ten fresh targets were brought forward, and every sound was hushed as the archers took their places once more.

This time the shooting was more speedily done, for only nine shafts were shot by each band. Then the judges came forward again and, looking at the targets, called aloud the name of each archer chosen as the best bowman of his band. Of these, Gilbert of the White Hand led, for six of the ten arrows he shot had lodged in the center. Stout Tepus and young Clifton came close upon his heels, while the others stood a fair chance for second or third place.

Amid the roaring of the crowd, those ten stout fellows who were left went back to their tents to rest for a while and change their bowstrings. Then while the deep buzz and hum of talking sounded all around like the noise of the wind, Queen Eleanor turned to the king and said, "Do you think these yeomen are the best archers in all merry England?"

"Yes, truly," said the king, smiling, for he was well pleased with the sport he had seen. "And not only are they the best archers in all merry England, but in all the wide world beside."

"What would you say," said Queen Eleanor, "if I were to find three archers to match the best three yeomen of all your guard?"

"I would tell you there live not three archers in all the world to match Tepus and Gilbert and Clifton," said the king, laughing.

"Now," said the queen, "I know of three such yeomen, and I have seen them this very day. I would not fear to match them against any three that you choose."

At this, the king laughed loud and long. "If you will bring the three fellows you speak of, I will promise faithfully to give them free pardon for forty days, to come or to go wherever they please, nor will I harm a hair of their heads. Moreover, if they shoot better than my yeomen, they shall have the prizes for themselves according to their shooting. Now send for your archers right away. But first let the others shoot, and then I will match those that win against all the world."

"So be it," said the queen. Thereupon, beckoning to Richard Partington, she whispered something in his ear, and the page bowed and left the place, crossing the meadow to the other side of the range, where he became lost in the crowd. At this, all who stood around whispered to one another, wondering what it all meant, and what three men the queen was about to set against those famous archers of the king's guard.

The ten archers of the king's guard took their stand again, and the great crowd hushed. Slowly and carefully each man shot, and so deep was the silence that you could hear every arrow rap against the target. Then, when the last shaft had sped, a great roar went up. Once again Gilbert had lodged three arrows in the white; Tepus came second with two in the white and one in the black ring next to it; but stout Clifton had gone down and Hubert of Suffolk had taken the third place, for while both those two good yeomen had lodged two in the white, Clifton had lost one shot upon the fourth ring, and Hubert came in with one in the third.

All the archers around Gilbert's booth shouted for joy, tossing their caps and shaking hands with one another.

In the midst of all the noise and hubbub, five men came walking across the lawn toward the king's pavilion. The first was Richard Partington, who was known to most folk there, but the others were strangers to everybody. Beside young Partington walked a yeoman clad in blue, and behind came three others, two in Lincoln green and one in scarlet. This last yeoman carried three stout bows of yew tree, two fancifully inlaid with silver and one with gold. While these five men came walking across the meadow, a messenger came running from the king's booth and summoned Gilbert, Tepus, and Hubert to go with him. Now the shouting ceased, for all saw that something unusual was about to happen, so everyone leaned forward to see.

When Partington and the others came to where the king and queen sat, the four yeomen bowed and doffed their caps to her. The queen leaned forward and said in a clear voice. "Locksley," said she, "I have made a wager with the king that you and two of your men can outshoot any three that he can send against you. Will you do your best for my sake?"

"Yes," said Robin Hood, "I will do my best for your sake, and if I fail, I promise never to finger bowstring again."

Now the king turned to the queen and said, "Who are these men that you have brought before us?"

The Bishop of Hereford, who once had been an unwilling guest of Robin's under the greenwood tree, spoke hastily, for he could hold his peace no longer. "Your Majesty," said he, "the fellow in blue is a certain outlawed thief of the midcountry, named Robin Hood; the tallest man goes by the name of Little John; the other fellow in green is Will Scarlet; the man in red is a rogue named Allan a Dale."

The king's brows drew together darkly, and he turned to the queen. "Is this true?" he asked sternly.

"Yes," said the queen, smiling. "The bishop has told the truth. But bear in mind that you promised safety of these good yeomen for forty days."

"I will keep my promise," said the king, in a deep voice that showed the anger in his heart, "but when these forty days are gone let this outlaw look to himself, for then things may not go as smoothly with him as he would like." Then he turned to his archers, who stood near the Sherwood yeomen, listening and wondering at all that passed. "Gilbert, and you, Tepus, and you, Hubert, I have pledged that you shall shoot against these three fellows. If you outshoot the knaves, I will fill your caps with silver pennies. If you fail, you shall lose your prizes that you've won so fairly. Do your best, lads, and if you win this bout you shall be glad of it to the last days of your lives."

Then the three archers of the king turned and went back to their booths, and Robin and his men went to their places from which they were to shoot. They strung their bows, looked over their quivers of arrows, and chose the roundest and the best feathered.

But when the king's archers went to their tents, they told their friends all that had passed, and how these four men were the famous Robin Hood and three of his band. The news of this buzzed among the archers in the booths, for there was not a man there who had not heard of these great men. From the archers the news was taken up by the crowd, so at last everybody stood up, craning their necks to catch sight of the famous outlaws.

Six fresh targets were set up, one for each man. Gilbert, Tepus, and Hubert came out from the booths. Then Robin Hood and Gilbert of the White Hand tossed a farthing aloft to see who should lead in the shooting, and the lot fell to Gilbert's side. He called upon Hubert of Suffolk to lead.

Hubert took his place, planted his foot firmly, and fitted a fair, smooth arrow. Breathing upon his fingertips, he drew the string slowly. The arrow sped true, and lodged in the white; again he shot, and again he hit the target; a third shaft he sped, this time missing the center yet striking the black, not more than a finger's breadth from the white. At this a shout went up, for it was the best shooting that Hubert had done that day.

Merry Robin laughed and said, "You will have a rough time bettering that round, Will, for it is your turn next. Bring not shame upon Sherwood."

Then Will Scarlet took his place. Because of over-caution, he spoiled his shot with the first arrow, for he hit the next ring to the black, the second from the center. At this Robin bit his lips. "Lad, lad," said he, "hold not the string so long!" To this Will Scarlet took heed, so the next arrow he shot lodged fairly in the center ring; again he shot, and again he smote the center; but, for all that, Hubert had outshot him. Then everyone clapped for joy because Hubert had beaten the stranger.

Said the king grimly to the queen, "If your archers shoot no better than that, you are likely to lose your wager." But Queen Eleanor smiled, for she looked for better things from Robin Hood and Little John.

Now Tepus took his place to shoot. He also was nervous, and so he fell into Will Scarlet's error. The first arrow he struck into the center ring, but the second missed its mark and smote the black; the last arrow was tipped with luck, for it smote the center.

Said Robin Hood, "That is the sweetest shot that has been sped this day. But nevertheless, friend Tepus, your cake is burned. Little John, it is your turn next."

Little John took his place and shot his three arrows quickly. He never lowered his bow arm in all the shooting, but fitted each shaft with his longbow raised; yet all three of his arrows smote the center within easy distance of the black. At this no sound of shouting was heard, for although it was the best shooting that had been done that day, the folk of London Town did not like to see the stout Tepus overcome by a fellow from the countryside, even if he were as famous as Little John.

Now stout Gilbert of the White Hand took his place and shot with the greatest care; and again, for the third time in one day, he struck all three shafts into the target.

"Well done, Gilbert!" said Robin Hood, clapping him upon the shoulder. "You are one of the best archers I ever saw. You should be a free and merry ranger like us, lad, for you are better fitted for the greenwood than for the cobblestones of London Town." So saying, he took his place and drew a fair, round arrow from his quiver, which he turned over and over before fitting it to his bowstring.

The king muttered, "Now, blessed Saint Hubert, if you will jog that rogue's elbow so as to make him smite even the second ring, I will give a hundred sixty wax candles to light your chapel." But Saint Hubert's ears must have been stuffed with wax, for he seemed not to hear the king's prayer.

Having gotten three shafts to his liking, merry Robin looked carefully to his bowstring before he shot. "Yes," said he to Gilbert, who stood near him to watch his shooting, "you should pay us a visit at merry Sherwood." Here he drew the bowstring to his ear. "In London"—here he loosed his shaft—"you can find nothing to shoot at but rooks and crows. In Sherwood one can tickle the ribs of the noblest stags in England." So he shot while he talked, yet the shaft lodged not more than half an inch from the very center.

"By my soul!" cried Gilbert. "Are you the devil in blue, to shoot that way?"

"No," said Robin, laughing, "not quite as bad as that." He took up another shaft and fitted it to the string.

Again he shot, and again he struck his arrow close to the center; a third time he loosed his bowstring and dropped his arrow just between the other two and into the very center, so that the feathers of all three were ruffled together, seeming from a distance to be one thick shaft.

And now a low murmur ran all among that great crowd, for never before had London seen such shooting as this, and never would see it again after Robin Hood's day had gone. All saw that the king's archers were fairly beaten, and stout Gilbert clapped his palm to Robin's, admitting that he could never hope to draw such a bowstring as Robin Hood or Little John.

But the king, full of anger, would not have it so, though he knew in his mind that his men could not stand against those fellows. "No!" cried he, clenching his hands upon the arms of his seat. "Gilbert is not yet beaten! Did he not strike the target three times? Although I have lost my wager, he has not yet lost first prize. They shall shoot again, and still again, till either he or that knave Robin Hood comes off the best. Go you, Sir Hugh, and bid them shoot another round, and another, until one or the other is overcome." Then Sir Hugh, seeing how angry the king was, said never a word, but went to do his bidding. He went to where Robin Hood and the other stood and told them what the king had said.

"With all my heart," said merry Robin, "I will shoot from now till tomorrow if it can pleasure my most gracious lord and king. Take your place, Gilbert lad, and shoot."

So Gilbert took his place once more, but this time he failed, for his shaft missed the center ring by not more than the breadth of a straw.

"Your eggs are cracked, Gilbert," said Robin, laughing; and he loosed a shaft, and once more smote the white circle of the center.

The king arose from his place and said not a word. It would have been an ill day for anyone he saw with a joyous or merry look upon his face. He and his queen and all the court left the place, but the king's heart was brimming with anger.

After the king had gone, all the yeomen of the archer guard came crowding around Robin, Little John, Will, and Allan, to snatch a look at these famous fellows. Thus it happened that the yeomen, to whom Gilbert stood talking, were all surrounded by a crowd of people that formed a ring about them.

After a while Gilbert, the chief of the yeomen, spoke to Robin and said, "According to the agreement, the first prize belongs rightly to you; so here I give you the silver bugle, here the quiver of ten golden arrows, and here a purse of fifty golden pounds." As he spoke he handed those things to Robin, and then turned to Little John. "To you," he said, "belongs the second prize, one hundred of the finest harts that run on Dallen Lea. You may hunt them whenever you like." Last of all he turned to stout Hubert. "You," said he, "have held your own against the yeomen, and so you have earned third prize." Then he called upon the other seven of the king's archers who had last shot and gave them each eighty silver pennies.

Then Robin said, "This silver bugle I keep in honor of this shooting match; but you, Gilbert, are the best archer of all the king's guard, and to you I freely give this purse of gold. Take it, man, and I wish it were ten times as much, for you are a right yeoman, good and true. Furthermore, to each of the ten who last shot I give one of these golden shafts apiece. Keep them always so that you may tell your grandchildren that you are the best yeomen in all the world." At this all shouted aloud, for it pleased them to hear Robin speak so of them.

Then Little John said, "Good friend Tepus, I don't want those harts of Dallen Lea, for in truth we have more than enough in our own country. I give them to you for your own shooting."

At this another great shout went up, and many tossed their caps aloft, and swore among themselves that no better fellows ever walked the earth than Robin Hood and his stout yeomen.

While they shouted, a tall man of the king's guard came forward and plucked Robin by the sleeve. "Good master," said he, "a young page, one Richard Partington, gave me a message for you from a certain lady. The message is: 'The lion growls. Beware your head.'"

"Is that so?" said Robin, starting. For he knew right away that it was the queen who sent the message, and that she spoke of the king's wrath. "I thank you, good fellow, for you have done me greater service than you know." Then he called his three yeomen together and told them privately that they had best be going, for it was likely to turn bad for them in London Town. So, without tarrying longer, they made their way through the crowd and left London Town.

The Chase of Robin Hood

SO ROBIN HOOD and the others left the archery range at Finsbury Fields and set forth on their journey home. It was well for them that they did, for they had not gone more than three or four miles when six yeomen of the king's guard came bustling among the crowd that still lingered, seeking Robin and his men, to seize them and make them prisoners.

It was poor form for the king to break his promise. But it was the Bishop of Hereford who counseled him to do so, for he spoke ill of Robin Hood to the king. And so it was that the king lent his ear to his evil counsel, until, after a while, he turned to Sir Robert Lee and ordered him to send six of the yeomen of the guard to take Robin Hood and his three men prisoners.

Sir Robert Lee was a gentle and noble knight, and he felt grieved to see the king break his promise. Nevertheless, he said nothing, for he saw how bitterly the king was set against Robin Hood. But Sir Robert Lee did not send the yeomen right away, but went first to the queen and told her all that had passed, and asked her to send word to Robin of his danger. So when, after a while, the yeomen of the guard went to the archery field, they did not find Robin and the others.

The afternoon was nearly gone when Robin Hood, Little John, Will, and Allan set forth upon their way home, trudging along merrily through the yellow light, which speedily changed to rosy red as the sun sank low. The shadows grew long and finally merged into the grayness of twilight. The round moon was floating up in the eastern sky when they saw before them the twinkling lights of Barnet Town, some ten miles from London. Down they walked through the stony streets and so came at last to a little inn. Robin Hood stopped, for the spot pleased him, and he said, "Here we will rest for the night, for we are far enough away from London Town and our king's wrath."

The men entered and ordered the inn's finest food and drink. After they finished their feast, the landlord came in and said that there was someone at the door, a certain young squire, Richard Partington, of the queen's household, who wished to speak to the man in blue without delay. Robin arose quickly and, bidding the landlord not to follow him, left the others gazing at one another, wondering what was about to happen.

When Robin came out of the inn, he found Richard Partington sitting upon his horse in the white moonlight, awaiting his coming.

"What news do you bring, Sir Page?" said Robin. "I trust that it is not of an ill nature."

"Well," said Partington, "it is ill enough. The king has been bitterly stirred up against you by that vile Bishop of Hereford. He sent men to arrest you at Finsbury Fields, but not finding you there, he has gathered his men and is sending them along this very road to Sherwood, either to take you prisoner or prevent you from getting back to the woodlands again. He has given the Bishop of Hereford command over these men. Two bands of horsemen are already upon the road, not far behind me, so you had best be gone from this place right away, for if you stay any longer, you are likely to sleep this night in a cold dungeon. This is the message the queen has told me to bring to you."

"Now, Richard Partington," said Robin, "this is the second time you have saved my life, and if the proper time ever comes I will show you that Robin Hood never forgets these things. As for that Bishop of Hereford, if I ever catch him near Sherwood again, things will not go well with him. You may tell the good queen that I will leave this place without delay, and will let the landlord think we are going to Saint Albans. But when we are upon the highroad again, I will go one way through the country and will send my men the other, so that if one falls into the king's hands the others may escape. We will go by devious ways, and so, I hope, will reach Sherwood in safety. And now, Sir Page, I bid you farewell."

Robin Hood went back inside and found his yeomen sitting in silence, waiting his coming. The landlord also was there, for he was curious to know what Master Partington had to do with the fellow in blue. "Up, my merry men!" said Robin. "This is no place for us, for there are men after us with whom we will stand but an ill chance if we fall into their hands. So we will go forward once more, nor will we stop this night till we reach Saint Albans." Taking out his purse, he paid the landlord, and so they left the inn.

When they had come to the highroad outside the town, Robin stopped and told them all that had passed between Partington and himself, and how the king's men were after them. He told them they should part company. Three would go to the east and he to the west, and thus, skirting the main highroads, they would come by different paths to Sherwood. And so they parted company.

Not long after this, twenty or more of the king's men came clattering to the door of the inn at Barnet Town. They leaped from their horses and quickly surrounded the place, the leader of the band and four others entering the room where the yeomen had been. But they found that their birds had flown again, and that the king had been foiled a second time.

"I thought they were bad fellows," said the host, when he heard whom the men-at-arms sought. "But I heard that blue-clad knave say they would go straight to Saint Albans. If you hurry, you may catch them on the high-road between here and there." The leader of the band thanked the host and, calling his men together, mounted and set forth again, galloping to Saint Albans on a wild goose chase.

After Little John, Will Scarlet, and Allan a Dale had left the highway, they traveled east without stopping. They next turned north and came through Cambridge and Lincolnshire. Then, striking to the west and the south, they came at last to the northern borders of Sherwood Forest, without meeting a single band of the king's men. Eight days they had journeyed before reaching the woodlands in safety, but when they got to the greenwood glade, they found that Robin had not yet returned.

For Robin was not as lucky in getting back as his men had been, as you shall hear.

After having left the great northern road, he turned to the west, and so came past Aylesbury to fair Woodstock. There he turned north, traveling a great distance till he came to Dudley. Seven days it took him to journey thus far. When he thought he had gotten far enough north, he took byways and grassy lanes instead of the main roads toward Sherwood, until he came to a place called Stanton. Now Robin's heart began to laugh aloud, for he thought that his danger had passed, and that his nostrils would soon smell the spicy air of the woodlands once again. But there is "many a slip betwixt the cup and the lip," which Robin soon was to discover.

When the king's men found themselves foiled at Saint Albans, and that Robin and his men were not to be found, they did not know what to do. Soon another band of horsemen came, and another, until all the moonlit streets were full of armed men. Between midnight and dawn another band came to the town, and with them came the Bishop of Hereford. When he heard that Robin Hood had once more slipped out of the trap, he stayed not a minute, but gathering his bands together, he pushed forward to the north, leaving orders for all the troops that came to Saint Albans to follow after him.

On the evening of the fourth day, he reached Nottingham Town, and there he divided his men into bands of six or seven and sent them all through the countryside, blocking every highway and byway to the east and the south and the west of Sherwood. The Sheriff of Nottingham called forth all his men likewise, and joined with the Bishop, for he saw that this was his best chance of paying back his score in full to Robin Hood.

Will Scarlet, Little John, and Allan a Dale had just missed the king's men to the east, for the very next day after they had passed the line and entered Sherwood the roads through which they had traveled were blocked. Had they tarried, they would surely have fallen into the bishop's hands.

Of all this Robin knew nothing. He whistled merrily as he trudged along the road beyond Stanton, with his heart free from care. At last he came to where a little stream flowed across the road. Here Robin stopped and, kneeling down, cupped his hands and began to drink. On either side of the road stood tangled thickets of bushes and young trees, and it pleased Robin's heart to hear the birds singing there, for it made him think of Sherwood.

All of a sudden, as he drank, something hissed past his ear and struck into the gravel and water beside him. Quick as a wink Robin sprang to his feet, and at one bound crossed the stream and the roadside and plunged headlong into the thicket, for he knew well that what had hissed past his ear was a gray goose shaft, and that to delay so much as a moment meant death.

As he leaped into the thicket, six more arrows rattled among the branches after him, one of which pierced his doublet, and would have struck deeply into his side but for the tough coat of steel he wore. Up the road came riding some of the king's men. They leaped from their horses and plunged into the thicket after Robin. But Robin knew the ground better than they did, so crawling here and stooping there he left them far behind, coming out, at last, upon another road about eight hundred paces distant from the one he had left.

Here he stood for a moment, listening to the distant shouts of the seven men as they beat up and down in the thickets like hounds that had lost the scent of the quarry. Buckling his belt more tightly around his waist, he ran down the road toward Sherwood.

Robin had not gone more than three furlongs in that direction when he came suddenly to the top of a hill and saw beneath him another band of the king's men, seated in the shade along the roadside in the valley beneath. Seeing they had not caught sight of him, he turned and ran back from where he had come, knowing that it was better to run the chance of escaping the men who were in the forest than to rush into the arms of those in the valley.

So back he ran, when the seven men came forth into the open road. They raised a great shout when they saw him, such as a hunter gives when the deer breaks cover, but Robin was then a quarter of a mile away from them, coursing over the ground like a greyhound. He never slackened his pace, but ran along, mile after mile, till he approached Mackworth, near Derby Town. Here, seeing that he was out of present danger, he sat beneath a hedge where the grass was the longest and the shade the coolest, to rest and catch his breath. "By my soul, Robin," he said to himself, "that was the narrowest miss you ever had in all your life."

Robin Hood's journey from London had been hard and long. He decided to travel on without stopping until he reached Sherwood. But he felt his strength giving way. He sat down and rested, but knew that he could go no farther that day, for his feet felt like lumps of lead.

Once more he arose and went forward. After traveling a couple of miles he came to an inn and asked the landlord to show him to a room. There were only three bedrooms, and to the worst of these the landlord showed Robin Hood. Robin cared little for the looks of the place, but he could have slept that night upon a bed of broken stones. Stripping off his clothes, he rolled into the bed and was asleep almost before his head touched the pillow.

Not long after Robin fell asleep, a great storm struck. More guests came to the inn to escape the storm. The landlord showed them to the two other rooms, and they settled in for the night. Then again the door opened and in came a friar of Emmet Priory. He called to the landlord for a meal and a room. The meal was delicious, and soon the friar had left on his plate not even enough to feed a mouse.

At last the friar bade the landlord show him to his room. But when he heard that he was to bed with Robin, he was as grouchy a fellow as you could find in all of

England. But there were no other choices. When he came to the room where Robin lay, he slipped of his clothes and climbed into bed, where Robin, grunting and grumbling in his sleep, made room for him. Robin was more soundly asleep than he had been for many a night, or he would never have rested so quietly with someone so close beside him. As for the friar, had he known who Robin Hood was, he would almost as soon have slept with a snake as with the man he had for a bedfellow.

The night passed comfortably enough, but at the first dawn of day Robin opened his eyes and turned his head upon the pillow. How he gaped and stared, for there beside him lay a friar! Robin pinched himself sharply but, finding he was awake, sat up in bed, while the other slumbered as peacefully as though he were safe and sound at home in Emmet Priory.

"Now," said Robin to himself, "I wonder how this man dropped into my bed during the night." So saying, he arose softly, so as not to waken the other, and looking about the room he spied the friar's clothes lying upon a bench near the wall. First he looked at the clothes, and then he looked at the friar. Said he, "Good Brother Whatever-thy-name-may-be, as you have borrowed my bed so freely I'll borrow your clothes in return."

He put on the holy man's garb, but kindly left his own clothes in their place. Then he went forth into the freshness of the morning, and the stableman asked Robin whether he wanted his mule brought from the stable.

"Yes, my son," said Robin, even though he knew nothing about the mule, "and bring it forth quickly, for I am late and must be going." Soon the stableman brought forth the friar's mule, and Robin mounted it and went on his way rejoicing.

As for the friar, when he arose he was in as pretty a stew as any man in the world, for his rich, soft robes were gone, likewise his purse with ten golden pounds in it, and nothing was left but Robin's clothes. He raged and swore, but his swearing fixed nothing and the landlord could not aid him. Moreover, because he had to be at Emmet Priory that morning upon matters of business, he had to put on Robin's clothes and be on his way on foot, without his mule.

Even then his troubles were not over, for he had not gone far before he fell into the hands of the king's men, who marched him off to the Bishop of Hereford. In vain he swore he was a holy man, but it was all for nothing because the bishop believed him to be Robin Hood.

Meanwhile, merry Robin rode along contentedly, passing safely by two bands of the king's men, until his heart began to dance within him because of the nearness of Sherwood. So he traveled on to the east, until all of a sudden he met a noble knight in a shady lane. Robin checked his mule and leaped from off its back.

"Well met, Sir Richard of the Lea," cried Robin, "for I would rather see you than any other man in England this day!" He told Sir Richard all that had befallen him, and now at last he felt himself safe, being so near to Sherwood again.

But Sir Richard shook his head sadly. "You are in greater danger now, Robin, than you have ever been," said he, "for bands of the Sheriff's men block every road and let none pass through without examining them closely. I know this, having passed them just now. Before you lie the Sheriff's men, and behind you the king's men, and you cannot hope to pass either way, for by now they will know of your disguise and will be in waiting to seize you."

Having spoken, Sir Richard bent his head in thought, and Robin felt his heart sink. Sir Richard spoke again, saying, "One thing you can do, Robin, and one thing only. Go back to London and throw yourself upon the mercy of our good Queen Eleanor. Come with me to my castle. Take off these clothes and put on clothes like those my men wear. Then I will go to London Town with a troop of men behind me, and you shall mingle with them, and thus will I bring you to where you may see and speak with the queen. Your only hope is to get back to Sherwood, for there none can catch you, and you will never get to Sherwood any other way."

Robin went with Sir Richard of the Lea and did as he said, for he saw the wisdom of the knight's plan, and that this was his only chance of safety.

Queen Eleanor walked in her royal garden, and with her walked six of her ladies-in-waiting. All of a sudden a man leaped up to the top of the wall from the other side and dropped lightly upon the grass within. All the ladies-in-waiting shrieked, but the man ran to the queen and knelt at her feet, and she saw that it was Robin Hood.

"Why, Robin!" she cried. "Do you dare to come into the very jaws of the raging lion? Alas, poor fellow! You are lost indeed if the king finds you here. Do you not know that he is seeking you throughout all of England?"

"Yes," said Robin, "I know the king seeks me, and therefore I have come. For surely no ill can befall me when he has pledged his royal word to Your Majesty for my safety. Moreover, I know Your Majesty's kindness and gentleness of heart, and so I lay my life freely in your gracious hands."

"I know that I have not protected you as I should have done," said the queen. "Once more I promise you my aid, and I will do all I can to send you back in safety to Sherwood Forest. Stay here till I return." She left Robin in the garden and was gone a long time.

When she came back, Sir Robert Lee was with her, and the queen's cheeks were hot, as though she had been talking with angry words. Sir Robert came to Robin Hood and spoke to the yeoman in a cold, stern voice. Said he, "Our gracious sovercign the king has tempered his anger toward you, and has once more promised that you shall depart in peace and safety. Not only has he promised this, but in three days he will send one of his pages to go with you and see that no one blocks your journey back.

"You may be thankful that you have such a good friend in our noble queen, for if not for her persuasion and arguments, you would have been a dead man. Let this peril that you have escaped teach you two lessons. First, be more honest. Second, be not so bold in your comings and goings. A man who walks in the darkness as you do may escape for a time, but in the end he will surely fall into the pit. You have put your head in the angry lion's mouth, and yet you have escaped by a miracle. Do not try it again." So saying, he turned and left Robin and was gone.

For three days Robin abided in London in the queen's household. At the end of that time came the king's head page, Edward Cunningham, and taking Robin with him, they departed north upon their way to Sherwood. Now and then they passed bands of the king's men coming back again to London, but none of those bands stopped them, and so at last they reached the safety of the sweet, leafy woodlands.

King Richard Comes to Sherwood Forest

SOME MONTHS PASSED since these adventures befell Robin Hood. During this time, King Henry died, and the throne passed to King Richard of the Lion's Heart. Now all Nottinghamshire was caught up in a mighty stir and tumult. King Richard was making a royal progress through merry England, and everyone expected him to come to Nottingham Town in his journeying. Messengers went riding back and forth between the Sheriff and the king, until at last the time was fixed upon when His Majesty was to stop in Nottingham, as the guest of the Sheriff.

And now came more bustle than ever, for the folk were building great arches across the streets, beneath which the king was to pass, and were draping these arches with silken banners and streamers of many colors. Even more was going on in the guildhall of the town, for here a grand banquet was to be given to the king and the nobles of his train, and the best master carpenters were busy building a throne where the king and the Sheriff were to sit at the head of the table, side by side.

It seemed to many of the good folk as if the day that should bring the king into the town would never come, but the day finally arrived. The sun shone down brightly on the stony streets, which were alive with a restless sea of people. On either side of the road, great crowds of town and country folk stood packed as close together as dried herring in a box, so that the Sheriff's men could hardly press them back to leave space for the king's riding.

"Take care whom you push against!" cried a great, tall man in friar's robes to one of these men. "Would you dig your elbows into me, sir? If you do not treat me with more respect, I will crack your skull, even though you be one of the mighty Sheriff's men."

At this a great shout of laughter arose from a number of tall yeomen in Lincoln green that were scattered through the crowd thereabouts. But one who seemed of more authority than the others nudged the man with his elbow. "Peace, Friar Tuck," he said. "Did you not promise me before you came here that you would be mindful of your words?"

"Yes," grumbled the other, "but I did not think to have a hard-footed knave trampling all over my poor toes as though they were no more than acorns in the forest."

Just then all arguing ceased, for the sound of many bugles came winding down the street. All the people craned their necks, and the crowding and the pushing grew greater than ever. Now a gallant array of men came gleaming into sight, and the cheering of the people ran down the crowd as fire runs in dry grass.

Heralds in velvet and cloth of gold came riding forward. Over their heads fluttered a cloud of snow-white feathers, and each herald bore in his hand a long silver trumpet, which he blew upon. From each trumpet hung a heavy banner of velvet and cloth of gold, with the royal arms of England emblazoned there. After these came riding noble knights, two by two, all fully armed. In their hands they bore tall lances, from the tops of which fluttered pennants of many colors and devices.

Behind these came a great array of men-at-arms, with spears and halberds, and, in the midst of these, two riders side by side. One of the horsemen was the Sheriff of

Nottingham. The other, who was a head taller than the Sheriff, was clad in a rich but simple garb, with a broad, heavy chain about his neck. As he rode along he bowed to the right hand and the left, and a mighty roar of voices followed him as he passed, for this was King Richard.

Then, above all the tumult, a great voice was heard roaring, "Heaven and its saints bless you, our gracious King Richard!" The king saw a tall, burly priest standing in front of the crowd with his legs wide apart as he backed against those behind.

"By my soul, Sheriff," said the king, laughing, "you have the tallest priests in Nottinghamshire that I ever saw in all my life. That man would make the great stone statues rub their ears and listen to him. I wish I had an army of such men as him."

To this the Sheriff answered not a word, but all the blood left his cheeks, and he grabbed the pommel of his saddle to keep himself from falling. For he also saw the fellow that had shouted, and knew him to be Friar Tuck, one of Robin Hood's men. Behind Friar Tuck he saw the faces of Robin Hood, Little John, Will Scarlet, Will Stutely, Allan a Dale, and others of the band.

"How now," said the king, "are you ill, Sheriff, that you grow so pale?"

"No, Your Majesty," said the Sheriff. "It was nothing but a sudden pain that will soon pass by." He said this because he was ashamed that the king should know that Robin Hood feared him so little that he dared to come within the very gates of Nottingham Town.

Thus rode the king into Nottingham Town on that bright afternoon, and none rejoiced more than Robin Hood and his merry men to see him come so royally to his people.

That evening, after the great feast in the guildhall at

Nottingham Town was done, a thousand waxen lights gleamed along the board at which sat lord and noble and knight and squire. At the head of the table, on a throne all hung with cloth of gold, sat King Richard with the Sheriff of Nottingham beside him.

Said the king to the Sheriff, laughing as he spoke, "I have heard much about the doings of certain fellows hereabouts, a certain Robin Hood and his band, who are outlaws and abide in Sherwood Forest. Can you tell me something of them, Sir Sheriff? For I hear that you have met with them more than once."

At these words the Sheriff of Nottingham looked down gloomily, and the Bishop of Hereford, who was present, scowled and chewed his bottom lip. Said the Sheriff, "I can tell Your Majesty but little concerning the doings of those evil fellows, except that they are the boldest law-breakers in all the land."

Then young Sir Henry of the Lea, a great favorite of the king, said, "May it please Your Majesty, I heard many stories from my father about this Robin Hood. If Your Majesty would like, I will tell you some of this outlaw's adventures."

The king laughed and urged him to tell his tales. When Sir Henry of the Lea was done, others there, seeing how the king enjoyed this merry tale, told other tales concerning Robin and his merry men.

"By the hilt of my sword," said King Richard, "this is the boldest man I have ever heard of. I must take this matter in hand and do what you could not do, Sheriff. I will clear the forest of him and his band."

That night the king sat in the place set apart for his lodging while in Nottingham Town. With him were young Sir Henry of the Lea and two other knights and three barons of Nottinghamshire. But the king's mind still dwelled upon Robin Hood. "Now," said he, "I would give a hundred pounds to meet this bold fellow, Robin Hood, and to see some of his doings in Sherwood Forest."

Sir Hubert of Gingham spoke, laughing, "Your Majesty's wish is not hard to satisfy. If Your Majesty is willing to lose one hundred pounds, I can arrange for you to not only to meet this fellow, but to feast with him in Sherwood."

"Sir Hubert," said the king, "this pleases me well. But how will you arrange for me to meet Robin Hood?"

"My plan is simple," said Sir Hubert. "Let Your Majesty and all of us here put on the robes of the Order of Black Friars, and let Your Majesty hang a purse of one hundred pounds beneath your gown. Then let us ride from here to Mansfield Town tomorrow. If I am not mistaken, we will all meet with Robin Hood and dine with him before the day is over."

"I like your plan, Sir Hubert," said the king merrily, "and tomorrow we will try it and see if it works."

So it happened that when early the next morning the Sheriff came to where his king was staying, the king told him what merry adventure they planned to have that morning. When the Sheriff heard this, he struck his forehead with his fist. "Alas!" said he, "what evil advice have you been given! My gracious lord and king, you know not what you do! This villain Robin Hood has no respect for either the king or the king's laws."

"But did I not hear right when I was told that this Robin Hood has shed no blood since he was outlawed?"

"Yes, Your Majesty," said the Sheriff, "you have heard right. Nevertheless—"

"Then," said the king, interrupting the Sheriff's speech, "what have I to fear in meeting him, having done him no harm? Truly, there is no danger in this. Perhaps you would like to go with us, Sir Sheriff."

"No," said the Sheriff hastily, "Heaven forbid!"

Now seven habits such as Black Friars wear were brought, and the king and those about him put them on, and His Majesty hung a purse with a hundred golden pounds in it beneath his robes. Then they all went forth and mounted the mules that had been brought to the door for them. The king told the Sheriff be silent as to their plan, and so they set forth upon their way.

Onward they traveled, laughing and jesting, until they passed through the open country and came within the forest itself. They traveled in the forest for several miles without meeting anyone, until they had come to that part of the road that lay nearest to Newstead Abbey.

"By the holy Saint Martin," said the king, "I wish I had a better head for remembering things of great need. Here have we come away and brought not so much as a drop of anything to drink with us. Now I would give half a hundred pounds for something to quench my thirst."

No sooner had the king so spoken than out from the side of the road stepped a tall fellow with yellow beard and hair and a pair of merry blue eyes. "Truly, holy brother," said he, laying his hand upon the king's bridle rein, "it were an un-Christian thing not to answer your plea. We keep an inn nearby, and for fifty pounds we will not only give you a fine drink, but we will give thee as noble a feast as you ever had." So saying, he put his fingers to his lips and blew a shrill whistle. Immediately the bushes and branches on either side of the road swayed and crackled, and sixty broad-shouldered yeomen in Lincoln green burst out of the trees.

"Who are you, you bold man?" asked the king. "Have you no regard for such holy men as we are?"

"Not a bit," said merry Robin Hood. "As for my name, it is Robin Hood, and you may have heard it before."

"Away with you!" said King Richard. "You are a bold fellow and a lawless one as well, I have heard. Let me and my companions travel on in peace."

"It may not be," said Robin, "for it would not look good of us to let such holy men travel onward with empty stomachs. But I'm sure you have a fat purse to pay your bill at our inn, since you offered so much for a drink. Show me your purse, holy man, or I may have to strip off your robes to search for it myself."

"No, that is not necessary," said the disguised king sternly. "Here is my purse, but do not put your lawless hands upon our person."

"My goodness," said merry Robin. "What proud words are these? Are you the King of England, to talk to me like that? Here, Will, take this purse and see what lies inside."

Will Scarlet took the purse and counted out the money. Then Robin told him to keep fifty pounds for themselves, and put fifty back into the purse. This he handed to the king. "Here, brother," said he, "take this half of your money, and thank Saint Martin, upon whom you called before, that you have fallen into the hands of such gentle rogues that they will not take all you have. But will you not pull back your hood? I would like to see your face."

"No," said the king, drawing back, "I may not pull back my hood, for my companions and I have vowed that we will not show our faces for twenty-four hours."

"Then keep them covered in peace," said Robin. "Far be it from me to make you break your vows."

So he called seven of his yeomen and told them each to take a mule by the bridle. Turning their faces toward the depths of the woodlands, they journeyed onward until they came to the open glade and the greenwood tree.

Little John, with sixty yeomen at his heels, had also gone forth that morning to wait along the roads and bring a rich guest to Sherwood, for many men with fat purses traveled the roads at this time, when such great doings were going on in Nottinghamshire. But though Little John and so many others were gone, Friar Tuck and forty more yeomen were seated or lying around beneath the great tree, and when Robin and the others came they leaped to their feet to meet him.

"By my soul," said merry King Richard, when he had gotten down from his mule and stood looking about him, "you have a fine group of young men around yourself, Robin. I think King Richard himself would be glad of such a bodyguard."

"These are not all of my fellows," said Robin proudly, "for sixty more of them are away on business with my good right-hand man, Little John. But, as for King Richard, I tell you, brother, there is not a man of us who would not pour out our blood like water for him. We yeomen love our king right loyally for the sake of his brave doings, which are so like our own."

Presently a great barrel was brought, and drinks were poured out for all the guests and for Robin Hood. Then Robin held his cup aloft. "Here is to good King Richard of great renown, and may all enemies against him be stopped."

Then all drank to the king's health, even the king himself. "I am surprised at your toast, good fellow," the king said to Robin.

"It's true," said merry Robin, "for I tell you that no one is more loyal to our lord the king than we men of Sherwood. We would give up our lives for his benefit."

At this the king laughed and said, “Perhaps King Richard’s welfare means more to me than you know. But enough of that matter. We have paid well for our fare, so can you not show us some merry entertainment? I have heard that you are wondrous archers. Will you show us your skill?”

“With all my heart,” said Robin. “We are always pleased to show our guests all the sport that is to be seen. Go, my merry men, grab your bows and set up the target.”

Quickly the men set the mark at which they were to shoot one hundred twenty paces distant. The target was a garland of leaves and flowers two spans wide, hung upon a stake in front of a broad tree trunk. “Now,” said Robin, “each of you shoot three arrows at the target.”

First David of Doncaster shot, and lodged all three of his arrows within the garland. “Well done, David!” cried

Robin. Next Midge the Miller shot, and he also lodged his arrows in the garland.

Thus the band shot, each in turn. Last of all, Robin took his place, and all was hushed as he shot. The first shaft he shot split a piece from the stake on which the garland was hung; the second lodged within an inch of the other. "By my kingdom," said King Richard to himself, "I would give a thousand pounds for this fellow to be one of my guard!" And now for the third time Robin shot; but alas for him! The arrow was ill-feathered, and wavering to one side, it smote an inch outside the garland.

At this a great roar went up, those of the yeomen who sat upon the grass rolling over and shouting with laughter, for never before had they seen their master so miss his mark. Robin flung his bow on the ground with vexation. "Now, wait a minute!" he cried. "That shaft had a bad feather on it, for I felt it as it left my fingers. Give me a clean arrow, and I will split the wand with it."

At these words the yeomen laughed louder than ever. "Nay, good uncle," said Will Scarlet in his soft, sweet voice, "you had a fair chance and missed. I swear the arrow was as good as any that has been loosed this day. You should face punishment for being such a poor sport."

"It may not be," said merry Robin. "I am king here, and no subject may raise his hand against the king. But I will give myself to this holy friar and take any punishment from him." Then he turned to the king. "I ask you, brother, will you give me my punishment with your holy hands?"

"With all my heart," said merry King Richard, rising from where he was sitting. "I owe you for having lifted a heavy weight of fifty pounds from my purse. So make room for him on the green, lads."

"If you knock me down," said Robin, "I will give you back your fifty pounds. But if you do not lay me on my back in the grass, I will take every penny you have for your boastful speech."

"So be it," said the king. "I am willing to risk it." And so he rolled up his sleeve and showed an arm so strong and well-muscled that it made the yeomen stare. But Robin stood with his feet wide apart, firmly planted, waiting and smiling. The king swung back his arm and delivered a blow like a thunderbolt. Down went Robin headlong upon the grass, for the blow would have felled a stone wall.

Then how the yeomen shouted with laughter till their sides ached, for never had they seen such a blow given in all their lives. As for Robin, he soon sat up and looked all around him, as though he had dropped from a cloud and landed in a place he had never seen before. After a while, still gazing at his laughing yeomen, he put his fingertips softly to his ear and felt all around it tenderly. "Will Scarlet," he said, "count this fellow out his fifty pounds. I want nothing more of his money or of him. I believe he has made this ear deaf, and I will never hear from it again."

Then, while gusts of laughter still rocked from the band, Will Scarlet counted out the fifty pounds, and the king dropped it back into his purse again. "I thank you, good fellow," said the king, "and if you should ever wish for another blow to the ear to match the one you have, come to me and I will give you one for nothing."

Suddenly there came the sound of many voices, and out from the trees burst Little John and sixty men, with Sir Richard of the Lea in their midst. Across the glade they came running, and as they came, Sir Richard shouted to Robin, "Make haste, dear friend, gather your men together and come with me! King Richard left Nottingham Town this very morning to find you in the woodlands. Now hurry with all your men, and come to Castle Lea, for there you may lie hidden till the present danger has passed. Who are these strangers you have with you?"

"Why," said merry Robin, rising from the grass, "these are gentle guests who came with us from the highroad over by Newstead Abbey. I do not know their names, but I have become well acquainted with this rogue's palm this morning. The pleasure of this acquaintance has cost me a deaf ear and fifty pounds to boot!"

Sir Richard looked keenly at the tall friar, who, drawing himself up to his full height, looked straight back at the knight. Sir Richard's cheeks grew pale, for he knew who it was. Quickly he leaped off his horse's back and flung himself upon his knees before the other.

At this, the king, seeing that Sir Richard knew him, threw back his hood, and all the yeomen saw his face and knew him also, for there was not one of them who had not been in the crowd in Nottingham and seen him riding side by side with the Sheriff. Down they fell upon their knees, nor could they say a word. The king looked all around grimly, and, last of all, his glance came back and rested again upon Sir Richard of the Lea.

"How is this, Sir Richard?" he said sternly. "How dare you step between me and these fellows? And how dare you offer your Castle of the Lea for a refuge to them? Will you make it a hiding place for the most famous outlaws in England?"

Then Sir Richard of the Lea raised his eyes to the king's face. "Far be it from me," said he, "to do anything that could bring Your Majesty's anger upon me. Yet sooner would I face Your Majesty's wrath than suffer any harm that I could keep from falling upon Robin Hood and his band. For to them I owe life, honor, everything. Should I, then, desert him in his hour of need?"

As the knight finished speaking, one of the mock friars who stood near the king came forward and knelt beside Sir Richard, and throwing back his hood showed the face of young Sir Henry of the Lea. Then Sir Henry grasped his father's hand and said, "Here kneels one who has served you well, King Richard. I stand by my dear father and say also that I would freely give shelter to this noble outlaw, Robin Hood, even though it brought your anger upon me, for my father's honor and my father's welfare are as dear to me as my own."

King Richard looked from one kneeling knight to the other. The frown faded from his face, and a smile twitched at the corners of his lips. "Well, Sir Richard," said the king, "you are a bold-spoken knight, but your freedom of speech does not bother me. Rise all of you, for you shall suffer no harm from me this day, for it would be a pity that a merry time should end in any way that would destroy its joyousness."

Then all arose and the king beckoned Robin Hood to come to him. "Now," he said, "is your ear still too deaf to hear me speak?"

"I would have to be dead before my ears would cease to hear Your Majesty's voice," said Robin.

"Do you think so?" said the king sternly. "Now I tell you that but for three things—my mercifulness, my love for a bold woodsman, and the loyalty you have sworn for me—your ears might indeed be closed forever in death. Do not speak lightly of your sins, good Robin. But come, look up. Thy danger is past, for I pardon you and your men from all you have done. Yet I cannot let you roam the forest as you have done in the past. Therefore I will take you at your word, when you said you would give your service to me, and you shall go back to London with me. We will take bold Little John also, and likewise Will Scarlet, and the minstrel, Allan a Dale. As for the rest of your band, we will take their names and have them recorded as royal rangers. For I think it is far wiser to have them changed to law-abiding caretakers of our deer in Sherwood than to leave them to run at large as outlaws. Get a feast ready. I would like to see how you live in the woods."

So Robin told his men to make ready a grand feast. Great fires were kindled and burned brightly, at which savory things roasted. While this was going on, the king asked Robin to call Allan a Dale so he could hear him sing. All listened in silence. When Allan a Dale had finished, King Richard sighed. "I tell you this, Allan, you have a sweeter voice than any minstrel I have ever heard."

Now someone came forward and said the feast was ready. Robin Hood brought King Richard to where it lay all spread out on fair white linen cloths upon the soft grass. King Richard sat down and feasted and drank, and when he was done he swore that he had never had such a tasty meal in all his life.

That night the king lay in Sherwood Forest upon a bed of sweet green leaves, and early the next morning he set forth from the woodlands for Nottingham Town. Robin Hood and all of his band went with him. You may guess what a stir there was in the good town when all these famous outlaws came marching through the streets. As for the Sheriff, he did not know what to say nor where to look when he saw Robin Hood in such high favor with the king, while his heart was filled with bitterness.

The next day the king left Nottingham Town. Robin Hood, Little John, Will Scarlet, and Allan a Dale shook hands with all the rest of the band, promising they would often come to Sherwood and see them. Then each mounted his horse and rode away in the train of the king.

THUS ENDS the merry adventures of Robin Hood. For in spite of his promise, it was many a year before Robin saw Sherwood again.

After a year or two at court, Little John came back to Nottinghamshire, where he lived in a quiet way, within sight of Sherwood, and where he achieved great fame as the champion of all England with the quarterstaff. Will Scarlet after a time returned to his own home. The rest of the band did their duty well as royal rangers.

Robin Hood and Allan a Dale did not come again to Sherwood so soon. Robin, through his fame as an archer, became a favorite with the king, so he quickly rose to be the chief of all the yeomen. At last the king, seeing how faithful and how loyal Robin was, named him Earl of Huntingdon. Robin followed the king to war and found his time so full that he had no chance to come back to Sherwood for even a day. As for Allan a Dale and his wife, the fair Ellen, they followed Robin Hood and shared in all his ups and downs of life.

And now, dear friend, we also must part, for our merry journey has ended.